A Sky-Blue Bench

Written by **Bahram Rahman**   Illustrated by **Peggy Collins**

pajamapress

First published in Canada and the United States in 2021

Text copyright © 2021 Bahram Rahman
Illustration copyright © 2021 Peggy Collins
This edition copyright © 2021 Pajama Press Inc.
This is a first edition.
10 9 8 7 6 5 4 3 2 1

www.pajamapress.ca   info@pajamapress.ca

 Canada Council for the Arts   Conseil des arts du Canada   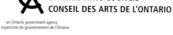 ONTARIO ARTS COUNCIL CONSEIL DES ARTS DE L'ONTARIO   an Ontario government agency   un organisme du gouvernement de l'Ontario   Canadä

The publisher gratefully acknowledges the support of the Canada Council for the Arts and the Ontario Arts Council for its publishing program. We acknowledge the financial support of the Government of Canada through the Canada Book Fund (CBF) for our publishing activities.

Library and Archives Canada Cataloguing in Publication

Title: A sky-blue bench / written by Bahram Rahman ; illustrated by Peggy Collins.
Names: Rahman, Bahram, 1984- author. | Collins, Peggy, 1975- illustrator.
Description: First edition.
Identifiers: Canadiana 20210241020 | ISBN 9781772782226 (hardcover)
Classification: LCC PS8635.A4175 S49 2021 | DDC jC813/.6—dc23Publisher Cataloging-in-Publication Data (U.S.)

Publisher Cataloging-in-Publication Data (U.S.)

Names: Rahman, Bahram, 1984-, author. | Collins, Peggy, 1975-, illustrator.
Title: A Sky-Blue Bench / written by Bahram Rahman ; illustrated by Peggy Collins.
Description: Toronto, Ontario Canada : Pajama Press, 2021. | Summary: "Young Aria returns to school after recovering from an accident and being fitted with a prosthetic leg, but the school has no furniture and sitting on the floor is too painful. She finds a way to build her own bench, surprising and inspiring her classmates. A sensitive author's note addresses the author's experience growing up in Afghanistan during the civil war and the legacy of landmines"— Provided by publisher.
Identifiers: ISBN 978-1-77278-222-6 (hardcover)
Subjects: LCSH: Artificial legs – Juvenile fiction. | Children with disabilities -- Juvenile fiction. | Resilience (Personality trait) – Juvenile fiction. | BISAC: JUVENILE FICTION / Disabilities & Special Needs. | JUVENILE FICTION / People & Places / Asia. | JUVENILE FICTION / School & Education. | JUVENILE FICTION / Social Themes / Self-Esteem & Self-Reliance
Classification: LCC PZ7.1R346Sk | DDC [F] – dc23

Original art created digitally
Cover and book design—Lorena González Guillén

Printed in China by WKT Company

Pajama Press Inc.
469 Richmond St. E, Toronto, ON M5A 1R1

Distributed in Canada by UTP Distribution
5201 Dufferin Street Toronto, Ontario Canada, M3H 5T8

Distributed in the U.S. by Ingram Publisher Services
1 Ingram Blvd. La Vergne, TN 37086, USA

To the children of Afghanistan

—B.R.

For Azalea, your love is
changing the world already

—P.C.

Aria walked carefully behind a long line of excited girls. She looked down to admire her new red shoes and tugged at her dress to make sure her helper-leg was covered.

Aria got a helper-leg after she had an accident. She stayed in the hospital for a long time and rested at home. Now, she was ready to go back to school.

But her school, a mud-brick building, had no benches. During the war, all the wooden furniture had been burned to keep the houses warm. Aria was worried about sitting on the floor all day.

When Aria arrived at her classroom, the other girls were already seated on the blue tarp that covered the floor. The teacher pointed her to the back row where she could lean against the wall. Aria walked slowly, her face burning as she felt everyone's eyes on her helper-leg.

Aria thought about her can of sky-blue paint.
There was still plenty left.

"Yes," she said, with a smile as wide as the sky.
"We can build everything we need, together!"

Author's Note

Parts of this story come from my personal experiences growing up in Kabul, Afghanistan. In particular, I remember the spring of 1993, when my class had to build our own benches and desks. All of the wooden furniture had been used as firewood by **internally displaced** families sheltering in our school through the winter.

A few years before that, in the first grade, I attended a special presentation that taught us how to distinguish between **land mines** and toys. One type of land mine they showed us was brightly colored and looked like a butterfly. It was even called a "butterfly mine." Its design has a reputation for being particularly attractive to curious children.

Every week dozens of civilians in Afghanistan, many of them children like Aria, are injured or lose their lives to land mines or other **unexploded ordnance (UXO)**. These weapons were planted or dropped by airplanes and drones, then left behind in every corner of Afghanistan during the last four decades of war. It will take many more years to clear and dispose of them, but the work is being undertaken by organizations like The HALO Trust and the United Nations Mine Action Service (UNMAS).

A *Sky-Blue Bench* honors the resilience of Afghan children in the face of great personal loss and injury caused by land mines and UXO. Although Aria has limited resources, she—like many other children in Afghanistan—confronts life as it is and solves her problems with creativity and hard work. She won't give up until life is better for her and the people around her.

—Bahram Rahman

Internally displaced people have lost their homes due to a war or disaster and need a new place to stay. Unlike refugees, they are still within their home country.

Land mines are dangerous weapons that explode when someone steps on or near them. Often, when a war is over, land mines are left behind in the ground where it was fought.

Unexploded ordnance (UXO) are military ammunition that has failed to explode when used during conflicts or military training. They can explode accidentally later, even after many decades.

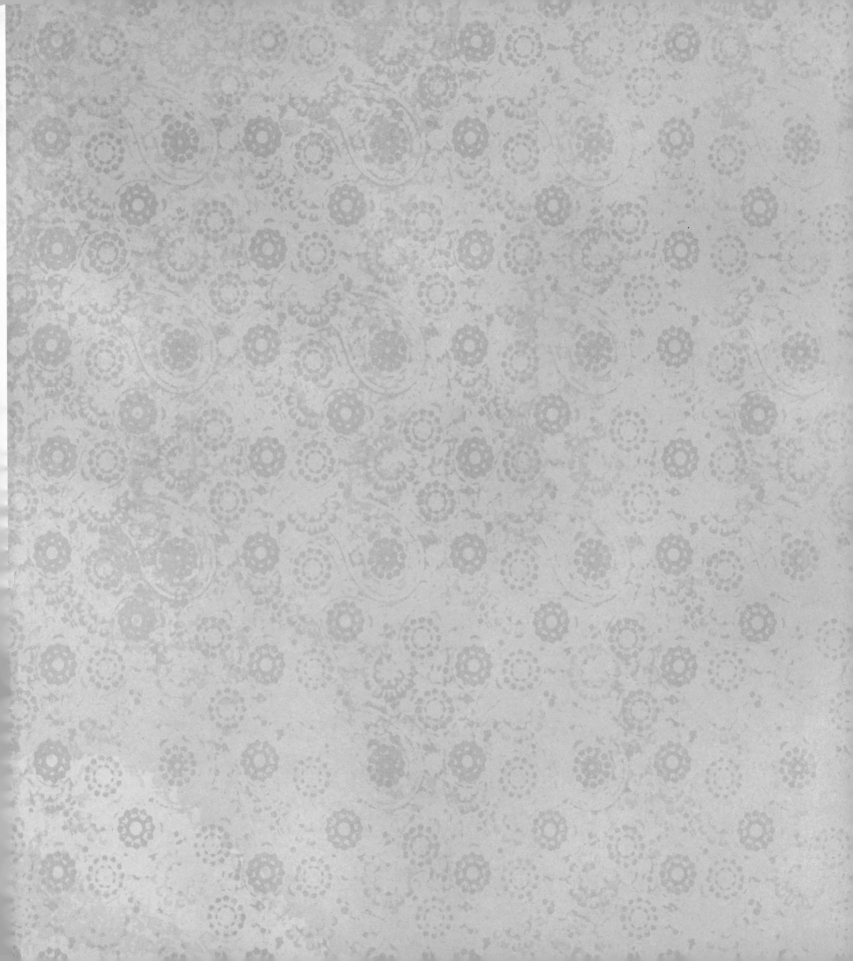